LIZZIE LIES A LOT

Elizabeth Levy

LIZZIE LIES A LOT

Illustrated by JOHN WALLNER

A YEARLING BOOK

Published by
Dell Publishing Co., Inc.
1 Dag Hammarskjold Plaza
New York, New York 10017

Text Copyright © 1976 by Elizabeth Levy
Illustrations Copyright © 1976 by John Wallner

Yearling ® TM 913705, Dell Publishing Co., Inc.
Reprinted by arrangement with Delacorte Press
ISBN: 0-440-44714-3
Printed in the United States of America
First Yearling printing—January 1977

To the memory of Bama
and
To Murray

LIZZIE LIES A LOT

1

Lizzie opened the door. She heard a woman's voice with a slight echo behind it saying, "Mark, you'll never understand me. You never did." Except for the sound of the television, the house was quiet. Lizzie knew right away that her mother wasn't home. Nana, her grandmother, sat slumped in a chair a few feet away from the set.

Lizzie put her books down in the hall. She looked in the mirror. Last year when she walked by this mirror she could only see the top of her head. Now her head and shoulders filled the bottom third of the mirror. Lizzie was nine.

Her arms seemed to be growing faster than any other part of her. They were long and skinny. Her face was small, making her large brown eyes look huge, but Lizzie never thought of herself as having pretty eyes. Her hair was both thin and fine. Her most recent haircut called for two barrettes to try to hold the ends together close to her ears. The barrettes pinched and hurt. Lizzie undid them and stuck them in her pocket.

When she turned away from the mirror, she found Nana looking at her. "I didn't hear you come in," Nana said. "You might have said hello."

Lizzie hated it when her grandmother had that hurt sound in her voice. "I thought maybe you were asleep," she said quickly. "Where's Mom?"

"She's at the thrift shop," replied Nana. Lizzie nodded. She had forgotten Wednesday was the day her mother volunteered at the hospital thrift shop. If she had remembered, she wouldn't have come home right from school.

Nana's thin arms pushed against her chair—arms as skinny as Lizzie's. She got up and walked toward Lizzie. Nana bent down and presented her cheek for a kiss. Lizzie's lips brushed Nana's cheek, which smelled too sweet from the old-fashioned face powder she used. Quickly Lizzie turned away.

Not quickly enough. Nana grabbed the elastic waistband of Lizzie's pants. Lizzie's shirt had ridden up, and was caught half in and half out of her pants. The edges of her undershirt hung unevenly below the shirt.

"You look like a wild baboon," said Nana, shoving the ends of Lizzie's shirt into her pants. "I don't know why your mother lets you go running around like that. You always look as if you're falling apart at the seams."

"Maybe I am a wild baboon . . . uhhh . . . huuu." Lizzie started to make grunting baboon noises.

"Don't be smart with me. Let me comb your hair." Nana fished in the pocket of her house-dress and pulled out an old comb. She used one hand to keep a tight grip on Lizzie's upper arm. With her other hand, she tried to untangle Lizzie's hair. Lizzie pulled her head away when Nana hurt her.

"Can't you stand still? You're wiggling like a worm," said Nana. She tightened her grip on Lizzie's arm. "Tell me what you did in school today," she demanded.

"First I'm a baboon; now I'm a worm. Worms and baboons don't go to school."

"Your smart mouth is going to get you in trouble," said Nana. "I asked what you did in school today."

"I was so popular that there was a fight at lunch because three people wanted to sit next to me. Ms. Cole had to break it up."

Nana looked doubtful. "Then," continued Lizzie, "Ms. Cole told me that I have the prettiest hair she had ever seen. She happens to love fine hair."

"Lies," muttered Nana. "I've never seen such a girl for telling lies. Some people are born liars."

Lizzie stopped wiggling around and became silent. "How do you know I'm lying?" she finally asked.

Nana gripped her arm even tighter. "A grandmother knows," she said.

Lizzie tried to shake her arm loose. "I've got something to do in my room," she said.

"You always hide in that room," muttered Nana, but she let her go. Lizzie rubbed her arm as she walked down the hall and shut the door to her room. Mrs. Kahn and Lizzie had recently redecorated the room. "You aren't a baby any more," Mrs. Kahn had said to Lizzie. They had bought a black-and-white tweed studio spread that made the bed look like a couch. Red and gold throw pillows perched on the bed in the corners. A long honey-colored wood desk and bookcase took up one wall. Another wall was lined with cork for Lizzie's drawings, most of which were of horses.

Once inside her room, Lizzie couldn't decide what to do. She sat on her bed, hugging her knees, glad to be away from her grandmother. She looked up at the picture of her favorite horse and began to imagine herself far away, riding in meadows below snow-capped mountains.

"Lizzie, I'm home . . . I'm home . . ." Mrs. Kahn drew out the word "home" into a long sound that echoed through the house.

"She's locked up in her room again," said Nana. "She was sassy and looked like a ragamuffin when she came in."

"Oh, you know Lizzie," said Mrs. Kahn lightly. "She always looks like she's going in two directions at once."

"Whose fault is that?" asked Nana. "If you took the time to look after her, maybe she wouldn't look like such a mess."

"All kids get messy," said Mrs. Kahn. She sounded tired. Three afternoons a week she worked as a volunteer at the hospital thrift shop. She liked the chance it gave her to get out of the house and do something useful. Mrs. Kahn was grateful that her mother was there to take care of Lizzie, but Nana always seemed to have some sort of complaint.

"I never let you go around looking like a rag-picker's daughter," continued Nana. "I didn't have the money you have, but I always saw to it that you looked nice."

"Kids are different today, Mother. I think Lizzie looks fine. You worry too much about how she looks. She's no messier than any of her friends."

"You don't pay any attention to how she looks," said Nana. "She's not the prettiest girl in the world, so it's important that she looks nice. It should be important to you." Nana emphasized the word "you."

"Mother, Lizzie is pretty," protested Mrs. Kahn. "Please, let's not argue about the way Lizzie looks again. Tell me, did you have a good afternoon?"

Nana looked hurt. "You don't care what kind of afternoon I had."

Mrs. Kahn sighed. "Of course I care." Her voice began to fade. Then abruptly she shouted, "Lizzie dear . . . come on out . . . I'm hoooome."

Lizzie had heard her the first time. In fact, she had been about to come out when she realized she could listen to her mother and grandmother talking, so she had stopped in the doorway. Now she ran down the hall and gave her mother a kiss. Hanging on the back of her mother's chair, she hopped up and down on one foot.

"Did you have a good day at school today?" asked Mrs. Kahn.

Lizzie nodded her head.

"Did anything special happen?"

"If you were home where you belong, you'd find out," muttered Nana under her breath.

Mrs. Kahn ignored her mother's comment. "Was there anything special about today?" she repeated.

Lizzie continued hopping, first on one foot, then on the other. She looked from Nana to her mother. "There's going to be a big Assembly soon," she said. "My teacher wants me to dance in it."

"How come I didn't hear anything about this?" asked Nana sharply.

"Uhhhmmmm, I forgot to tell you," said Lizzie. "You were watching TV, and then you started calling me a baboon and a worm."

"I never . . ." said Nana. "See, that's the way your child talks to me when you're not here."

"Lizzie, I'm sure Nana didn't call you a baboon," said Mrs. Kahn.

"She did," insisted Lizzie. "And she said I was a worm."

"I was just telling her what she looked like, for her own good," protested Nana. "It's better

she should know from someone who loves her
... a stranger isn't going to tell her the truth."

"I am not a worm," said Lizzie defiantly.

"Of course you're not," said Mrs. Kahn. "You
know Nana didn't mean it literally. Come on,
tell me about the dance at school. What part do
you play?"

"It's a big part," said Lizzie quietly.

"Tell me about it," persisted Mrs. Kahn. From the corner of her eye Lizzie saw Nana. Her mouth was set in a tight line. Suddenly Lizzie wanted to get out of the living room very badly. "I'll tell you about the dance later," she said quickly, trying to sound cheerful. "I've got to practice." As she walked to her room, Lizzie could hear her mother say, "See, Mama, Lizzie can't be such a mess if her teacher chose her to star in her dance Assembly. I'm so pleased. I knew all those lessons at dancing school would help her."

Lizzie closed the door to her room before she could hear Nana's reply. She turned on her record player so her mother would know she was practicing.

2

The next day at school, Lizzie and her best friend, Sara, hurried down the hall to gym class. Quickly they changed into their gym suits and went to sit in a circle with the rest of the girls from the fourth-grade class. Ms. Brinsmaid, the gym teacher, stood in the middle. She had straight blond hair, and her bangs hung in sharp little points on her forehead. "We're going to play dodgeball," she said. "I want a good game today. I want you girls to throw hard and look. Don't just close your eyes and hope you'll hit someone. Let me have Sara and Carol as captains."

As soon as Sara stood up, Lizzie wiggled to the left a few inches to fill up some of the space she had left. Lizzie always felt a slight twinge in her stomach when teams were chosen. She was never the last one picked, but almost.

Sara had first choice. "Mary!" she shouted out. Lizzie nodded her head in agreement. If she had been Sara she would have chosen Mary first too. Mary had big shoulders and stood nearly a head taller than everyone else.

Carol, the other captain, chose Dede. Dede was the best-coordinated girl in the class. Now it was Sara's turn again. Lizzie stared at the lines in the gym floor.

"Lizzie." Lizzie's head jerked up. Casually she uncrossed her legs and gave a half smile at Sara. Out of the corner of her eye Lizzie thought she saw Ms. Brinsmaid push her lips in and out impatiently. Ms. Brinsmaid did not like it when captains chose their friends instead of the best players.

Lizzie took her place in the lineup, wondering if Mary was mad at Sara for picking her. Ms. Brinsmaid said the team was only as strong as its weakest link. Lizzie looked up at Mary, who was whispering into Sara's ear. "Maybe," Lizzie thought, "she's telling her what a dope she was to choose me."

Lizzie shifted her weight from side to side. Her blue gym shorts had a grease spot on them. Lizzie looked down at it. She had forgotten to take her gym suit home to be washed four days in a row. Quickly she covered the spot with her hand so Ms. Brinsmaid wouldn't notice. It was right over her hipbone. Lizzie knew she looked silly standing there with her hand on her hip, but she didn't want Ms. Brinsmaid to notice the spot.

Finally the teams were chosen, and Ms. Brinsmaid blew her whistle. The eight girls on Sara's team spread out on their half of the floor. Two balls were in play at once. One was headed directly for Lizzie. She bounced on her toes and sucked her stomach in. The ball missed her by inches. It made a thud as it hit the padding and dribbled out on the floor. Lizzie picked it up and tossed it to Mary. Mary flung the ball, and one of the girls on Carol's team was out.

"Come on, kids," shouted Sara to her team. One ball whizzed by again. This time it wasn't aimed at Lizzie, and she started to yell, "Come on, team . . . let's go."

The two balls passed rapidly from side to side, catching girls on the legs, in the stomach, on the arms, on the backside. Soon Sara, Mary, and Lizzie were the only ones left on Sara's team. Lizzie had managed to stay in much longer than she usually did. Mary grabbed the ball as it bounced off the wall and handed it to Lizzie. Lizzie bounced it back to Mary.

"No, you take it," panted Mary. "I'm out of breath." Lizzie started to pass the ball to Sara, but Sara said, "No, your turn." Ms. Brinsmaid shouted at them to stop stalling. The volleyball was much bigger than Lizzie's hand. She tried to throw it one-armed, the way Mary did, but as she whirled around she left the ball behind her.

"Great shot," jeered Carol as the ball dribbled over to her side. Carol scooped the ball up and hit Lizzie hard, right in the abdomen. Lizzie went "Woof," as the air flew out of her. She walked to the side, holding her stomach. A few minutes later, Mary and Sara both were out and the game was over.

Sara and Mary walked over to Lizzie. "It was a great game," said Mary, grinning.

"I'm really sorry; I just dropped the ball," said Lizzie. "I ruined it."

"You were in there almost to the end," said Sara.

"Yeah, I was," said Lizzie happily.

"We'd better hurry," said Mary. "We've got to be at Assembly in about five minutes."

Lizzie's smile dissolved.

"What are you worried about?" asked Mary. "You really played a good game."

"That's not what I was thinking about," said Lizzie, who was thinking about another Assembly altogether. "Nothing's worrying me," said Lizzie. "Forget it."

3

When school was over, Lizzie and Sara got on their bikes. On their way home they passed a half-finished house.

"Hey," said Lizzie. "It looks like all the workmen have gone, let's explore." They walked their bikes over the deep ridges made by the trucks and the front-end loaders. The foundation of the house had been poured, and the vertical wooden frame was up. There were no front steps, but a hill had been made out of the dirt from the basement. Lizzie and Sara climbed the hill, then jumped over to the house. They were both skinny enough to slip through the two-by-fours.

"I bet this is going to be the living room," said Lizzie, walking around the front of the house.

"Here's the bathroom," said Sara, giggling. She pointed to a small room with a hole in the floor. Lizzie joined her. They walked through to the back of the house.

"This is sort of scary," said Sara. "Won't we get in trouble if we're caught?"

"No," said Lizzie. "We can always tell them that the house belongs to our uncle."

"What if the police ask us for the name of our uncle and try to call him?" insisted Sara in a worried voice. "It's probably not legal to be here."

"The police wouldn't want to lock up two little kids," said Lizzie. "They'd believe the story about our uncle."

"Maybe we should go," suggested Sara. "I'm not as good a liar as you are."

Lizzie looked up at Sara, a little surprised. Quickly she changed the subject.

"Let's look upstairs, just for a second. There's a ladder."

Lizzie started to climb first. Suddenly she

ducked her head, lost her balance, and slipped down a rung. One of her loafers came off and fell on Sara's head.

"Ouch!" cried Sara. "What's the matter?"

"I think there's a rat up there." Lizzie was breathing hard. "I heard a scurrying noise, and it sounded just like a rat."

"Let's get out of here!" yelled Sara. "*I hate rats!*"

"Me too! Just let me get my loafer on." Lizzie sat down on the sawdust to put on her shoe.

"Hurry up," cried Sara. "Rats can give you rabies, and then you have to have a bunch of shots in your stomach. Mary told me that." Sara waited impatiently until Lizzie had her loafer on before she jumped from the edge of the house. She landed on the dirt pile, lost her footing, and did a somersault down the hill, scraping her knee. She picked herself up and looked at her knee. Little horizontal lines of blood started to ooze out. She wiped the blood with her hand and looked around for Lizzie. She couldn't find her.

Lizzie had taken one last look up the stairs where she thought she had heard the rat. At the edge of the hole, where the ladder rested against the second-story floor, a small black-

and-white face peered down. The cat looked at Lizzie and gave a soft mew. Its hair was all matted, and the fur between its ears was gummy.

"*Lizzie!*" screamed Sara. "*Get out of there!*"

"It's not a rat!" shouted Lizzie. Her shout startled the cat, and it disappeared from the opening. "Now I scared it," she muttered to herself.

Lizzie walked to the edge of the house and called to Sara: "Come back. It was only a cat, and I want to find it. It looked starved."

"How do you know it wasn't a rat?" Sara asked doubtfully.

"I saw it," said Lizzie.

"Maybe it was a rat . . . a huge one, and you only thought it was a cat. Come on. Let's get out of here."

"No," insisted Lizzie. "It was a pretty cat."

Sara didn't say anything for a few seconds. "I scraped my knee," she said finally. "It hurts."

Lizzie looked at Sara's bloody knee. "Don't you want to come look for the cat?" she asked anxiously.

Sara shook her head. "I'm scared of rats. The idea of getting all those shots in the stomach makes me puke."

"O.K.," said Lizzie. "You go home. I'll look for the cat myself."

"You shouldn't play here by yourself," said Sara. "You could get hurt."

"I have to find that cat. It could be starving and need help."

Sara sat down on top of the mud hill and looked at her knee. "I'll wait here," she said finally.

Lizzie turned back into the house. She climbed the ladder and hoisted herself onto the upper floor. It wasn't completely finished, and she could easily fall through a hole if she didn't look where she was going.

"Here, kitty, kitty," she said softly. "I'm not going to hurt you. Come on, kitty."

There was no sound except Lizzie's voice.

"Please, kitty. Tell me where you are," she pleaded. She heard a sound near a large paper bag lying on the floor. Lizzie thought she saw the bag move.

"Is that where you are?" she asked. She walked over to the bag and squatted on her knees; slowly she lifted it. The cat hissed at her. It was even dirtier than she had first thought.

"I'm not going to hurt you," said Lizzie, and she sat on her haunches and didn't move. "You won't believe this," she said in a soft voice, "but when I heard you up here, I thought you were a rat."

The cat stopped hissing. Very slowly it moved one paw closer to Lizzie. It stood there poised, ready to run. Its head was cocked as it listened to Lizzie talk.

"I wonder if you did find any rats up here," Lizzie continued in the same soft voice. "I hope not. I'm just as scared of rats as Sara. I hate rats."

The cat took another step forward, and Lizzie held her hand out. She kept her fingers in a fist so the cat wouldn't think she was going to grab it. The cat sniffed her fist. It opened its mouth, and its scratchy sandpaper tongue licked Lizzie's second knuckle.

"Would you like to meet my friend Sara?" she asked. Slowly and steadily, Lizzie leaned forward and picked the cat up under the stomach. For a couple of seconds the cat struggled. "It's O.K., pussycat," Lizzie crooned. The cat settled into her arms, and she stroked its matted fur.

"What's happening?" asked Sara. She had come back into the house and was standing at the bottom of the ladder.

"Help me down," said Lizzie. "I've got the cat in my arms." Sara climbed halfway up and

guided Lizzie's feet down each rung. When they were at the bottom Lizzie showed the cat to Sara.

"Be very, very quiet," Lizzie whispered. "She's scared."

"She's pretty," said Sara, "even though she's all dirty."

"She's skinny. You should feel her. Her ribs stick out."

Sara patted the cat while Lizzie held her. "This is what I'm really like," whispered Lizzie. "Sometimes I act different and showoffy, but when I'm with animals I'm really me. I never lie when I talk to animals."

Sara looked uncomfortable but didn't reply. She kept stroking the top of the cat's head.

"I don't think she belongs to anybody," said Lizzie. "Let's go to my house and give her some milk."

They went outside, and Sara walked both bikes while Lizzie carried the cat. "Will your mom let you keep it?" asked Sara.

"Oh sure," said Lizzie. "Mom loves animals."

"Then how come you don't have a dog or cat or anything?"

Lizzie bent down and kissed the cat on top of its head. "Mom loves cats, but once she had one and it died a horrible death. She was so upset that she never got another one. She keeps saying it would make her too sad, but I'm sure she'll let me keep this one."

"How did the other cat die?" asked Sara.

Lizzie took a deep breath. She heard the words coming out, but she couldn't believe she was saying them. In a way, she wanted to stop, to take them back, but she knew she wasn't going to.

"When my mother was a little girl, a friend of my grandmother's was living with them. This woman was my grandmother's best friend. One day this woman saw my mom's cat and thought it was a tiger going to eat her up. She started wrestling with the poor beautiful little kitten, pulling the kitten's hair out with her bare hands. My mom kept screaming at her to stop, but she was just a little girl then, and the woman didn't pay any attention. She kept bashing the little kitten's head against the kitchen table . . ."

Sara stared at Lizzie incredulously. "You're making that up," she said.

"I am not," said Lizzie indignantly.

"I don't believe you," said Sara. "It's too horrible."

"Just because it's horrible doesn't mean it's not true. It gets worse. The woman kept bashing and bashing the kitten. My mother was screaming. I don't know where my grandmother was. I think she was out and she had left this crazy woman alone with my mom. By the time my grandmother came home, the kitten was dead, and my mom couldn't stop crying. That's why she never let me have any pets of my own. She never got over it. But I think it's going to be different this time."

"Was that story true?" demanded Sara.

Lizzie nodded her head, holding the kitten tightly.

"It really happened?" asked Sara doubtfully.

"It did," said Lizzie.

"It's the most horrible story I ever heard," said Sara, shivering. She wasn't sure whether to believe Lizzie.

4

"*Let's go* in the back way," said Lizzie when they got to her house. "I bet Nana is sleeping." The back door was open, and they could hear the sound of the television in the living room.

Lizzie put the cat down on the clean linoleum floor. She went to the refrigerator and poured some milk into a saucer. As she was lowering the saucer to the floor, the cat came and rubbed its body against her ankles. "I'm going to take care of you," whispered Lizzie. The cat began to lap up the milk.

A few seconds later the swinging door of the kitchen creaked. The cat looked up, startled. Its tail began to flick back and forth. "What's that animal doing in my kitchen?" demanded Nana. The cat's diamond-shaped eyes narrowed into slits. Its legs locked at the joints. Its back began to arch.

"We found her when we were playing," said Lizzie, picking up the cat. "She was starving."

"I thought you were practicing for your Assembly," said Nana.

"What Assembly?" asked Sara.

"I, uh . . . uhhh . . ." Lizzie stammered and looked over at Sara and decided to ignore her question. "Practice got canceled," she whispered to Nana in a hoarse voice.

"Why are you whispering?" demanded Nana.

Sara looked at Lizzie strangely. She was very confused.

"I'm whispering because I don't want to upset the cat," said Lizzie softly.

Nana focused on the cat. "It's filthy. You shouldn't pick up strange cats. You could get sick." Nana sounded worried and a little frightened. She took a step toward Lizzie to take the cat away. The cat hissed and struck its paw at Lizzie's arm. Bright red blood appeared in a straight line of tiny dots.

Nana sucked in her breath. "It's a wild animal. You're bleeding." Sara looked at the blood on Lizzie's arm. She didn't really understand what was going on between Lizzie and Nana.

Lizzie licked the blood off her forearm. The cat's fur brushed her mouth. "It's not a wild animal. This cat loves me. You just scared it."

"Loves you! It just scratched you. I want you to let go of that cat this minute," insisted Nana.

Sara spoke up and defended Lizzie. "It really isn't a wild cat. Lizzie carried it all the way home, and it seemed to like her."

Lizzie gave Sara a thankful look. The kitchen became quiet, and Sara felt very uncomfortable. "Maybe we should take the cat outside until your mom comes home," Sara suggested.

"I'm taking the cat outside for now," Lizzie said to Nana. "But when Mom comes home, she'll let me keep her."

"You're not going to keep that cat," warned Nana, but Lizzie had already backed out the door into the yard. Lizzie got a piece of clothesline and made a leash for the cat so it wouldn't run away. The cat began to clean itself, licking its paws rather slowly, as if the pads on the bottom of its paws hurt.

"Wow, was your Nana mad!" blurted out Sara.

"Don't worry about her," said Lizzie. "My mom will let me keep the cat."

"What Assembly were you supposed to be practicing for?" asked Sara.

"Oh, it's just something for my dance school. You know, that place where I take lessons. Hey, we've got to think of a name for my cat."

"How about Housecat, 'cause you found her in a house?"

"No, it sounds too much like 'houseboat.' I think I'll call her Princess, because she's so pretty."

"Princess is a good name," agreed Sara. "Do you think this cat looks like the one your mom once had?" Sara paused for a moment. "Was that story really true?" she asked, still not knowing whether to believe Lizzie.

Lizzie ignored Sara's question as she watched Princess clean herself. "She can't seem to get the matted part on her head. I'm going to get some soap and water so she'll be all neat and clean when my mom comes home. Wait here."

"I don't think cats like water," shouted Sara, but Lizzie was already back in the house. A few seconds later she came back with a bowl full of warm soapy water and a washcloth. Princess had finished washing herself. She cocked her head and looked at Lizzie suspiciously as Lizzie raised a dripping-wet washcloth over her head.

Suddenly Princess leaped into the air and bounded away, trailing the clothesline behind her. She dashed across the lawn, and Lizzie went after her. Just as the cat was about to disappear through the hedge, Lizzie made a lunge and managed to bring her foot down on the end of the clothesline.

Princess was brought up so short that she did a flip onto her back and got all tangled up in the rope. She fought furiously to get free.

"It's O.K., Princess, it's O.K. . . ." said Lizzie, her voice high and squeaky with excitement. She tried to unravel the leash from around the cat's legs, but Princess was in a panic. Each time Lizzie got one of her paws freed, she would get another paw tangled.

Sara came over to help. Princess's claws were extended as far as they could go. She was acting as if she were fighting for her life.

"Lizzie . . . what's going on?" Mrs. Kahn's voice floated over the lawn.

Lizzie and Sara stood in the far corner of the

lawn. They looked over at Mrs. Kahn. Their backs hid Princess.

"*Nothing!*" shouted Lizzie.

"What do you have there? Nana said something about a cat."

"Wait a minute!" shouted Lizzie.

Mrs. Kahn walked across the lawn gingerly, tiptoeing on the balls of her feet so that her high heels wouldn't make holes in the grass. "What's going on?" she insisted.

Princess was on her back, flailing her paws in the air. She seemed hopelessly entwined in the rope. Lizzie's arms were full of scratches from trying to get her free.

Mrs. Kahn finally got close enough to look over Lizzie's shoulder. "What are you doing to that cat?" she demanded.

"Hold on a second," Lizzie pleaded. She grabbed hold of the free end of the leash. Talking and crooning to Princess, Lizzie managed to soothe her so that she stopped fighting and let herself be untangled. Lizzie picked her up and stroked her, starting with the now hopelessly matted fur on the top of Princess's head.

"That cat is filthy," said Mrs. Kahn. "I don't think you should be holding it. Where did it come from?"

Princess lay quietly in Lizzie's arms. "She doesn't belong to anyone, but she loves me."

"Princess really likes Lizzie," volunteered Sara.

"I'm sure," said Mrs. Kahn. "But you can't just pick up a stray cat. It might be diseased. You could get terribly sick."

"She's a healthy cat," contradicted Lizzie. "You should have seen her run across the lawn. She's very healthy." Sara backed Lizzie up by nodding her head.

"We'd better call the pound. They can come pick it up," said Mrs. Kahn.

"You can't do that," cried Lizzie. "They kill cats at the pound. We've got to keep her. She's mine. There's something special between us."

"They really do kill stray cats at the pound," said Sara. "I know that's true. You wouldn't want this cat to die. It must have been awful for you when your kitten died."

"What kitten are you talking about?" asked Mrs. Kahn. Lizzie had put her finger to her lips, trying to caution Sara not to mention that horrible story, but Sara wasn't looking at Lizzie. She was looking very earnestly at Mrs. Kahn.

"The kitten that died when you were a child," explained Sara.

Mrs. Kahn looked very confused.

"Mom, I want to keep this cat," interrupted Lizzie. "I'll take care of her all by myself. Please, can't I keep her?"

"Sweetheart, you know you don't have time to take care of a cat. Look how busy you are.

You said yourself, most afternoons you're going to have to practice."

"I'd have time for the cat, Mom."

"Cats don't take very much time," said Sara. "I could help Lizzie take care of her."

"Won't you be busy with the Assembly too, dear?" asked Mrs. Kahn.

"I don't go to dancing school," replied Sara, but Mrs. Kahn didn't hear her because Lizzie had come running up and thrust Princess into her face.

"Look at her closely, Mom. See, she's really beautiful. You can pet her."

Mrs. Kahn took a step away. "You know I don't like cats," she said sharply.

Sara stood by herself, frowning. If Mrs. Kahn didn't like cats, it seemed unlikely that Lizzie's story had been true. Yet she couldn't believe that Lizzie would have made up such a horrible story. Sara hated it when she didn't know whether Lizzie was lying or not. "I guess I should be getting home," she said.

"I think that's a good idea," said Mrs. Kahn. "It's quite late, and I don't want your mother to worry." Lizzie could tell from the look on Sara's face that something was upsetting her. She was beginning to wish they had never found Princess. Then she felt Princess's warmth as she held her, and suddenly she felt everything would end up all right. She smiled at Sara reassuringly. "See you tomorrow, O.K.?"

Sara nodded her head, got on her bike, and rode off.

5

"*I'm going* inside to call the pound," said Mrs. Kahn. "They don't kill all the cats they get. They'll do what's best."

"This cat loves me, Mom," said Lizzie. "I could tell the moment we met. It was like ESP. You've gotta let me keep her. I love her."

"Don't talk nonsense. Cats don't love people. I've never liked cats. They always walk away from you."

Lizzie held on to Princess tighter. Behind her mother's back Lizzie could see Nana coming across the lawn.

"Look at her holding that filthy cat," cried Nana in a shrill voice.

Mrs. Kahn suddenly tensed. She turned and half faced her mother. Nana was hurrying across the lawn. "Let go of that cat right this minute," she demanded.

Lizzie took a step backward, away from both her mother and Nana. "No. I'm keeping this cat. She's mine."

Nana turned and faced Mrs. Kahn. "You're letting her keep that?"

"Mother, Lizzie isn't going to keep the cat. Don't get excited," said Mrs. Kahn wearily. She turned to Lizzie. "Be reasonable, sweetheart. You can't just bring home any stray animal you see off the street. We'd soon be overrun."

"We don't have *any* animals," said Lizzie. She sounded close to tears. "You keep telling me that we can't have a dog or cat because of Nana. But this isn't any stray animal. She was meant for me. I know it."

Mrs. Kahn looked exasperated. "Lizzie, you are not bringing that cat into the house and that's that. I've explained to you why we can't have a dog or a cat. Nana's already broken her hip once. We can't have an animal underfoot. It would be too dangerous."

"She doesn't care," said Nana. "What does she know about how painful a broken hip can be? All she cares about is a pet. You hear her all the time . . . please can't we have a dog . . . now she brings home a cat. She wants to kill me."

Lizzie buried her chin in the cat's fur. "I'll keep this cat out of your way," she said.

"Faaagh," said Nana.

"Lizzie, you are not bringing that cat into the house and that's that. You're away at school all day. You don't have time to take care of a cat. You don't want to give up your starring role in the Assembly, do you?"

"Sure," said Lizzie. "I'd much rather have the cat than dance in that dumb Assembly. I'll tell my teacher I can't be in the Assembly and you'll let me keep the cat. It's a deal."

"Don't be ridiculous. Dancing is much more important than that cat."

"Who knows what diseases are on that filthy cat," interrupted Nana.

"Cats are clean," shouted Lizzie. "They're cleaner than you are."

"See how she talks to me—see!" said Nana angrily.

"Elizabeth, apologize to your grandmother. I'm going to call the pound. We can't stand here all day."

Lizzie shook her head. "Can't we wait and ask Daddy if I can keep it? Please, Mom, please."

"There's nothing to be discussed. I don't like cats. It would be dangerous to have one around because of Nana's hip. And I didn't hear you apologize to your grandmother."

"I'm sorry, Nana," said Lizzie hurriedly. "But please don't call the pound till Daddy comes home," Lizzie pleaded. "Just wait . . . please . . . I'll sit outside with it until then."

"Lizzie, you are impossible." Mrs. Kahn turned and walked across the lawn into the house. Nana shook her head, glared at Lizzie, and followed Mrs. Kahn.

Lizzie sank down into the grass, tears falling from her eyes. "It's going to be O.K., Princess," she whispered. "My dad will understand. You'll live in my room, and you won't ever have to see anybody else. I'll bring you food, and we can play. You'll see."

It got darker. Lizzie sat on the cement stairs leading to the back door. Princess fell asleep in her arms. Every once in a while, as if she were dreaming, her tail flicked back and forth, gently tickling Lizzie's arm.

Finally a car turned into the driveway. When she heard the door slam, she called in a hoarse whisper, "Dad, come here!"

"What are you doing?" asked Mr. Kahn, peering through the semi-darkness.

"I love you, Dad," said Lizzie quietly.

"I love you too, sweetheart," said Mr. Kahn. "But what are you doing sitting out here? It's getting cold." Mr. Kahn sat on the step beside Lizzie. "What do you have there?" he asked, eyeing the black-and-white thing in Lizzie's arms.

"Shhh," said Lizzie. "She's sleeping. She's my cat. Her name is Princess. Isn't she beautiful?"

"Where did you get it?" asked Mr. Kahn in a whisper. "Who does it belong to?"

"I found her," said Lizzie. "She was nearly starving and scared, but now she feels much better." Princess opened her eyes. Mr. Kahn could see the light reflected in the dark yellow irises of the cat's eyes. Princess lay contentedly in Lizzie's arms. As Lizzie stroked her, she began a deep purr.

"She seems to like you," said Mr. Kahn.

"You can pet her, and, Daddy, her name is

Princess," said Lizzie. Mr. Kahn leaned over and stroked the cat along her back. The inside of his arm rested on Lizzie's shoulder. Lizzie settled in, enjoying his warmth. They sat there quietly for several moments.

Suddenly the bright floodlamps over them went on.

"David, is that you?" asked Mrs. Kahn. "I thought I heard your car. Then I couldn't imagine what happened to you."

"I'm just out here with Lizzie," said Mr. Kahn.

Mrs. Kahn opened the back door and stood over Lizzie and her father. Lizzie squinted in the light of the floodlamp. The cat's eyes narrowed, adjusting to the light.

"Does she still have that cat?" asked Mrs. Kahn. "She picked it up somewhere and just brought it home."

Mr. Kahn drew his arm slowly away from Lizzie so they were no longer touching.

"I want to keep it, Dad," said Lizzie, very quietly. "I'll keep it in my room, where it won't bother Mom or Nana. Mom wants to take it to the pound, and they'll kill it."

Mr. Kahn looked up at Mrs. Kahn. He looked perplexed.

"She can't keep the cat, David," insisted Mrs. Kahn. "A cat could be very dangerous with Nana's hip. Beside, Nana hates cats. So do I. And Lizzie was very rude to Nana this afternoon."

"I don't understand," said Mr. Kahn. "Where did this cat come from? Who does it belong to?"

"Nobody," said Lizzie. "Sara and I found her. She's starving, and she needs a home."

"David, we can't keep it," said Mrs. Kahn, ignoring Lizzie. "We'll have to take it to the pound."

Mr. Kahn stood up. Just then Nana came to the back door and looked out through the screen. "She's still out there with that cat, isn't she?" asked Nana. Nana stepped out onto the back step. It was very crowded, with Nana, Mr. Kahn, and Mrs. Kahn all standing within inches of one another and Lizzie sitting on the step below them. Lizzie felt as if there wasn't room to breathe.

Nana turned to Mr. Kahn. "Are you letting her keep that cat? It's probably full of diseases. She could get sick and die. We all could."

"Nana," said Mr. Kahn, "I'm sure Lizzie isn't going to catch a disease from that cat. Neither are we."

"Excuse me," said Nana in a hurt voice. "I thought maybe you might care a little about your child's health. I guess that's old-fashioned. It's probably a good experience for her to get so sick she might die like a dog."

"Mother, stop talking about Lizzie dying!" shouted Mr. Kahn.

"David, don't shout at my mother," cried Mrs. Kahn.

"I wasn't shouting," said Mr. Kahn.

"You were," said Mrs. Kahn. "Besides, we can't stand here on this back step forever. You've got to tell Lizzie to let us take that cat to the pound."

Mr. Kahn looked down at Lizzie, who was sitting silently, holding on to her cat. "Sweetheart, Mom's right," said Mr. Kahn gently. "We don't know anything about this cat. It might be vicious. It really might be sick. They'll take care of it at the pound, and we can't keep it. You know that."

Lizzie didn't lift her head. She opened her arms and pushed the cat off her lap with all her strength. The cat jumped off and took five steps. Then she turned her head and looked back at Lizzie. Her tail was twitching.

"I don't want the cat anyhow," said Lizzie.

"See, she ran away from me." The cat stood half in and half out of the shadow of the floodlight.

Mr. Kahn's eyes looked disturbed as he gazed down at Lizzie. "Sweetheart, it's probably for the best," he said.

6

That night, just before Lizzie was going to sleep, her mother came in to kiss her good night.

"You've been very quiet tonight," said Mrs. Kahn. "I know you're still upset about that cat, and I know you really want a pet, but it's too dangerous. Nana's not too steady on her feet since she broke her hip. We have to be careful of her."

Lizzie said nothing. Mrs. Kahn sat down on the bed. "I know you have a hard time getting along with Nana," she said sympathetically.

"Nana doesn't like me," said Lizzie softly.

"She loves you very much," said Mrs. Kahn.

"It's true, sometimes she doesn't show it. Sometimes when people get old they get irritable, but you should try not to let it bother you. Nana tries to show her love. She makes you special cookies and cakes."

Lizzie shook her head. "She never says anything nice to me."

Mrs. Kahn laughed nervously. "That's just her way, sweetheart. Nana thinks it's bad luck to give a compliment. It's an old superstition never to say anything nice to someone you love because it might bring bad luck. But I know she loves you. She's proud of you for many reasons. She and I were just talking about how wonderful it was that you were chosen for your dance Assembly."

Lizzie turned her eyes to the wall. Her stomach felt tied up in knots. She couldn't think of anything to say. Mrs. Kahn's fingers played with the edge of Lizzie's blanket. "I know Nana's not the easiest person to get along with . . . I'm her daughter, and even I have trouble sometimes. But she's old, and she needs us. And she loves us." Mrs. Kahn's voice trailed off as she looked at Lizzie, trying to see some response. "Try to understand how Nana feels sometimes. It's not easy to be getting old, with Papa dead

. . . no longer having a home of her own. And we need her too. She helps me and you . . . not just with the cooking and taking care of you. Nana's a good person to have around. She makes a lot of sense. Oh, I know, sometimes she can seem overwhelming, but she loves us all, a lot."

Lizzie turned and faced her mother. Tears filled the corners of her eyes. "Sweetheart," exclaimed Mrs. Kahn, "don't look so sad. Just promise me you'll try to get along with Nana."

Lizzie looked down. She didn't want to promise. If Nana didn't live with them, then Princess could have stayed. If Nana didn't live with them, she wouldn't have to listen to how awful she looked. If Nana didn't live with them, maybe her mother wouldn't go to the hospital thrift shop, and she'd be home when Lizzie came home from school. But Lizzie couldn't say any of those things. She was afraid to tell her mother how she felt about Nana, afraid that her mother would really be mad, maybe even hate her. So Lizzie promised to try to be nicer to Nana. Mrs. Kahn leaned over and kissed Lizzie good night. "Things will seem better in the morning," she said.

Lizzie lay in her bed, her eyes wide open.

Her room never got completely dark. The street light outside threw shadows on her ceiling. Lizzie stared at the ceiling. She cried silently . . . until the tears were streaming down her face, wetting her pillow, but she made no sound. She didn't want her mother or father to know she was crying. Finally she fell asleep.

At school the next morning, Sara ran up to Lizzie. "What happened?" she asked. "Did your mom let you keep the cat?"

Lizzie had been dreading seeing Sara. She looked around, hoping that maybe Princess was somewhere close by and she wouldn't have to admit the truth. "What happened?" Sara asked again.

Lizzie's eyes felt tired from all the crying she had done the night before. She blinked several times. "It's a complicated story," she said to Sara.

Sara was pretty sure that the Kahns had taken the cat to the pound, and that Lizzie felt terrible. She forgot how mad she was about Lizzie's lie and just felt sad. She could tell that Lizzie didn't want to say what happened. "They took her to the pound, didn't they?" she asked sympathetically.

"Oh, no," said Lizzie. At least that wasn't a lie. Princess had run away before her parents could take her to the pound.

"Did they let you keep her?" asked Sara, not quite believing that it could be true.

Lizzie took a deep breath. It was just too painful to tell the truth. A lie came out much easier. "My dad thought the cat was beautiful," she said, and paused. "He wanted me to keep her. Nana was the only one who didn't want me to have her."

"Your mom sure didn't act like she liked cats," said Sara, frowning. "She wanted to send her to the pound."

"After you left, the cat went into Mom's arms and snuggled there, just like she did when I held her. She purred, and Mom stroked her back." As Lizzie said the words, she pictured Princess in her mother's arms, and for a moment she actually felt as if it really had happened that way.

Sara looked doubtful. "She said she hated cats."

"But Princess was different. Mom and Dad both wanted me to keep her, but Nana has a broken hip, and we couldn't keep her."

"But what happened to the cat?" insisted Sara.

"Ohhh . . ." said Lizzie. She seemed far away. "In the end we had to give her away."

Sara looked disappointed. "Who did you give her to?"

"Uhmmmmm . . ." Lizzie thought hard. "My father has some friends in the country. Mom, Dad, and me drove the cat to the farm last night, even though it was late. We left Nana home. My father's friends are very nice. They gave us hot chocolate, and they had milk and cat food for the cat. The cat is going to stay out there, and I'll visit her." Lizzie's voice grew more and more cheerful as she talked.

"Can I come with you?" asked Sara, relieved. It all sounded true. "I'd like to see the cat again. She liked me."

"I don't know," said Lizzie slowly. "I asked my dad if we could take you, but he said that this couple once had a little girl named Sara and she died. She fell off a horse. He thought they might be upset if they saw another little girl named Sara."

"Come on, Lizzie, you're making that up," said Sara, feeling as if she had been tricked.

"No, it's true. Of course, we could take you if you had another name."

Sara looked thoughtful. After all, maybe it was true. Why should Lizzie lie about something like that? "What name do you think we should use?"

"It shouldn't even sound like Sara," said Lizzie. "How about Gladiola?"

"Gladiola!" repeated Sara.

"How about Pansy?" asked Lizzie.

"Pansy!" shrieked Sara. "I don't want to be called Pansy."

"How about English Muffin?" suggested Lizzie. "That's a good one. That doesn't sound anything like Sara. We can call you English for short."

"How about Raisin Toast?" suggested Sara. "Then you could call me Raisin for short."

"Or Melba Toast."

"I hate Melba toast."

"O.K. Butter Toast. Butter for short."

Sara started to giggle. Then the bell rang for class. Sara sat at her desk, but every time she thought of being called Butter or English or Raisin she started to giggle. When Lizzie saw Sara giggling, she would start too.

"Do Sara and Liz want to share their joke with the rest of us?" asked Ms. Cole.

Lizzie and Sara shook their heads.

"Are you sure?" Ms. Cole asked. "I like good jokes."

Lizzie and Sara both shook their heads again.

"O.K.," said Ms. Cole, smiling. "Let's keep private jokes for private times. Lizzie, will you please pass out the readers."

After school, Mary and Sara stood by their bicycles. "Come on over to my house," said Mary. "Sara's coming. We can play basketball in my back yard."

"I can't," said Lizzie. "There's something I've got to do." Before they could say anything, Lizzie got on her bike and rode off. She headed straight to the half-finished house. The workmen were still there. Lizzie felt shy and a little frightened, but she got up the courage to talk to them.

"Excuse me," she said. "Have you seen a black-and-white cat today?"

"There was one hanging around here for days," said one of the workmen. "Haven't seen it today, though. Was it yours?"

Lizzie nodded her head. It didn't seem like a lie. She felt as if Princess *were* hers.

"Hey, Bill," shouted the man. "Have you seen that black-and-white cat anywhere?"

"Not today," shouted a man in the house. "I was wondering where it had gone. Usually I give it part of my lunch. Did the owner show up?"

"Yeah, it belongs to this little girl. I'm sorry. It was here. We'll keep an eye out for it, and why don't you give us your name and number, and if we find it we'll give you a call."

Lizzie thought for a second. She couldn't give them her real name and number. "Our phone's out of order," she said. "But I'll come back tomorrow. If you find her you can keep her for me. O.K.?"

"Sure," said the man. "How did you happen to know she was here?"

"A friend of mine came by and thought she recognized Princess. Princess is her name."

"Well, I hope we find her for you," said the man.

"Thanks," said Lizzie. She turned and walked over to the vacant lot next to the construction site. She tramped through the stickers and high grass, hoping to see Princess. It was quite late in the afternoon, and the light was getting low. Lizzie waited until the last workmen had driven off; then she scrambled into the house. She sat down on the exact spot where she had found Princess. She closed her eyes and told herself that when she opened them again Princess would be there. She counted to one hundred slowly, then opened her eyes. The half-finished house was exactly as it was before. By now the sky was a deep pink. Lizzie stood up slowly and went home.

7

At dinner Lizzie picked at her food. She was having a hard time swallowing. Mr. Kahn looked at her sympathetically. "Aren't you hungry?" he asked.

"Not very," said Lizzie.

Mr. Kahn squinted and pursed his lips. Lizzie knew he did that only when he felt uncomfortable, and she felt glad. She wanted him to be uncomfortable.

"Are you angry because we wouldn't let you keep that cat?" he asked.

Lizzie played at her food moodily. She wished

he hadn't asked. She felt like screaming, "Yes, I'm angry," but she didn't dare.

Just at that moment, Nana reached across the table and plunked a big pile of mashed potatoes on Lizzie's plate. Lizzie looked up, startled. "I don't want any more," she said.

"Mother, why don't you ask Lizzie if she wants more before you give it to her," said Mr. Kahn.

"She'd only say no," replied Nana tartly.

"Why do you always talk to me like I'm not here?" asked Lizzie, secretly glad that she hadn't had to answer her father's question.

"What's she talking about?" asked Nana.

Lizzie saw Mr. Kahn start to laugh. Her mother tried to change the subject. "Did you have rehearsal for your Assembly?" she asked. "How is it going?"

"O.K.," said Lizzie. Her voice sounded very flat.

"Tell me more about it," insisted Mrs. Kahn.

"It's not that big a deal," said Lizzie.

"You were very excited about it the other day," said Mrs. Kahn. "You should have seen her, David. She was bubbling all over."

"What's the dance about?" asked Mr. Kahn, smiling. He too was glad to have the subject changed.

"Oh, it takes place long ago." Lizzie paused. Her parents looked at her expectantly. "Well..." Lizzie continued. "I play the princess, and I'm very, very brave. There's a war going on, and my father, the king, is killed. The queen is ready to give up, but I go to the court magician and he makes me a magic sword. I put on a helmet to hide my long, beautiful hair, and I go out to fight our enemies." As Lizzie spoke her voice grew more and more animated.

"The queen, my mother, is very upset when she finds out, but it's too late to do anything about it. A very handsome prince is leading the warriors on the other side. He and I have a terrible fight."

"Don't talk so much with your hands," interjected Nana. Lizzie was indeed gesturing wildly. She looked down at the pile of mashed potatoes and realized that she had lost her train of thought.

"Go on, dear," said Mrs. Kahn. "Finish the story."

Lizzie thought for a moment and went on. "Well, the prince and the princess fight. This is a terrific part of the dance. Finally, he knocks off the helmet and sees her long hair. He realizes she's a girl. He stops fighting and orders his men to stop. The princess has been wounded, and blood is gushing from her arms. He makes a bandage out of his shirt and carries the princess home.

"When the queen sees him, she bows down and offers to surrender the kingdom to the prince. The prince is very angry with her. He tells her that her daughter is the bravest girl he has ever met. He banishes the queen from the kingdom, and he decides to marry the princess and they will rule together."

Mr. Kahn was trying hard not to smile. "It sounds like a very complicated dance for a school Assembly," he said. "Who made it up?"

"Ms. Cole," said Lizzie. "But she says it was a ballet they used to do a long time ago in Russia."

"Lizzie," said her father, laughing. "Are you sure you're not making this up?"

"Of course I'm sure," she said indignantly. "It's going to be a beautiful dance. There are no words."

"David, you know those school pageants," said Mrs. Kahn. "They always have incredibly elaborate plots."

Mr. Kahn looked skeptical.

"Do you need a costume?" asked Nana. She sounded almost shy. "I could make you one."

"No," said Lizzie quickly. "Ms. Cole is making the costume."

"I could make you something beautiful. I'd like to."

"Ms. Cole wants to make mine herself because she wants it to be perfect," Lizzie answered.

"I won't force my costume down your throat," said Nana. She sounded hurt.

Mrs. Kahn got up from the table. "Who's ready for dessert?" she asked. "Nana baked a wonderful applesauce cake."

"Sounds good to me," said Mr. Kahn.

"I don't want any," said Lizzie.

"Look at her," said Nana. "She's too skinny as it is. Her arms are like toothpicks."

"I'm not hungry," said Lizzie, looking up at her father. "Can I be excused? I want to practice my dance."

Mr. Kahn looked thoughtful. "I guess so, but I like it when you sit with me while I have coffee."

Lizzie half slipped off her chair. "I really want to practice," she said.

"Well, if you have to practice, I guess you have to. Come give me a kiss." Lizzie put her arms around her father's neck and gave him a kiss and a hug. Mr. Kahn squeezed Lizzie tightly. "I love you, darling," he said.

Nana looked at them longingly, as if she hoped Lizzie would come to her and give her a kiss. Lizzie went into her room and closed the door.

8

A *week* went by. Lizzie made sure that Sara didn't visit her house once. She kept telling Sara she had things to do each afternoon. Then, late Friday afternoon, Mrs. Kahn knocked on Lizzie's door. Lizzie had the record player on, because she had told her mother she was practicing, so she didn't hear her mother's knock. Mrs. Kahn walked in. Lizzie was lying on her bed reading a book.

"Did you get tired of practicing?" asked Mrs. Kahn. Lizzie looked down. "Yes," she said, and quickly got up to turn off the record player.

"Sara's mother just called," said Mrs. Kahn.

"She has to go away for the day tomorrow, and she asked if Sara could come over here to play. Won't that be fun? I haven't seen Sara all week."

Lizzie didn't reply.

"I can't understand why you've been so silent and grumpy lately," said Mrs. Kahn. "Are you that nervous over this dance?"

"I guess so," said Lizzie hesitantly, "but, Mom..."

Mrs. Kahn had her hand on the doorknob. "What is it, Lizzie?" she asked.

Lizzie looked up into her face. "Nothing, Mom," she replied.

The next morning, Lizzie didn't feel well. She told her mother she had a sore throat. Mrs. Kahn felt Lizzie's forehead.

"I don't think you've got a fever," she said.

"I feel sick," said Lizzie.

Mrs. Kahn got a thermometer, put it in Lizzie's mouth, and left the room. As soon as she was gone, Lizzie ran into the bathroom and turned on the hot water. She held the thermometer under the faucet, and then ran back into bed and popped the thermometer back into her mouth just as she heard her mother's footsteps in the hall.

Mrs. Kahn smiled at Lizzie, took the thermometer, and looked at it. "It's below normal," she said, puzzled. "Are you sure you kept it in? Put it back under your tongue for another minute."

Mrs. Kahn sat on the bed while Lizzie lay with the thermometer in her mouth. "You're normal," said Mrs. Kahn, sounding pleased, after she looked at the thermometer a second time.

"I *feel* sick," said Lizzie. "I think I'm coming down with something. I don't think Sara should come over. She could catch it."

"Oh, I don't think you're contagious," said Mrs. Kahn easily.

Lizzie swallowed hard to show she had a sore throat, but her mother had already turned her back to leave the room. Lizzie lay in her bed, feeling trapped.

It was pouring out when Sara arrived at noon.

"Come to my room," said Lizzie. "I've got something to show you."

"Isn't your friend even going to say hello?" asked Nana, who was sitting in her armchair. Sara turned to say hello, but Lizzie was pulling on her arm. She half dragged Sara down the hall to her room. They were there only a few moments before Mrs. Kahn called them out to lunch.

Lizzie and Sara came to the table just as Mrs. Kahn finished pouring tomato soup into bowls.

"Hey, Butter, you want some toast?" asked Lizzie.

Sara started to giggle.

"Do you want some buttered toast?" Mrs. Kahn asked innocently.

Both Lizzie and Sara collapsed in giggles.

"What's so funny about buttered toast?" asked Mrs. Kahn with a smile.

Lizzie and Sara were laughing so hard that they couldn't talk. Nana sat down at the kitchen table with her soup. "You shouldn't let them laugh so hard when they're eating. It will give them indigestion."

"Indigestion!" shouted Lizzie. "That's what your name should be."

Sara laughed so hard that she spit out her soup. Little puddles of tomato soup lay all around her plate. Seeing this, Lizzie broke up completely.

"What's going on with you two giggle monsters?" asked Mrs. Kahn good-naturedly. Nana sat shaking her head back and forth, saying, "They're going to make themselves sick."

"Come on, you two," said Mrs. Kahn.

"Enough's enough. Stop laughing, and eat your soup like grown-ups."

Sara took her napkin and wiped up around her plate. She didn't dare look at Lizzie, because she knew they'd start laughing again. Lizzie stared straight into her bowl, but every few seconds she erupted in a giggle. Nana and Mrs. Kahn ate their meal in silence.

"We're going to go in my room to play," said Lizzie when they were finished eating.

"I have to go to the shop this afternoon," said Mrs. Kahn, "but Nana will be here if you girls want anything."

Lizzie and Sara went into her room and closed the door. "What are we going to do?" asked Sara. She stood by Lizzie's cork wall looking at all the pictures of horses. "Do you have any new games to play?"

"Let's play pretend," said Lizzie. "We're sisters, and we live out west on a ranch."

"O.K.," said Sara. "What do we do there?"

"We ride every day. We each have our own horse. One day, our father gets very sick. He'll die if we don't get a doctor. Our mother has to stay with him, but she's afraid to let us go to town because there is a gang of robbers hiding

76

out between our ranch and town. We sneak out of the house and ride for the doctor."

"And we meet the robbers, right?" asked Sara.

"They ambush us," said Lizzie. "You and I try to fight them off, but there are just too many of them. They carry us into their shack. They're really surprised that two girls can put up such a good fight. The robbers decide to kidnap us. They think our father has lots of money." Lizzie paused. "They tie us up. Let's act that part out. We can take the sheets from my bed."

Lizzie and Sara stripped Lizzie's bed and rolled the sheets into fat ropes. "Sit on my chair," commanded Lizzie. "I'll tie you up."

Sara sat down, and Lizzie wound the sheet around her forearms and across her chest. She tied it tight in the back of the chair. "Can you move?" she asked.

Sara wiggled around. "I can move a little," she said. "I think you'd better tie my feet. If those robbers left my feet free, I'd be able to walk around in the chair." Sara leaned forward and showed how she could put her feet on the ground and take a few steps with the chair tied to her back. As she did it, the sheet loosened. The chair slipped off Sara's back, knocking her forward, so that she ended up underneath it.

"The sheet's no good," said Sara, out of breath. "We need real rope."

"Wait here," said Lizzie. "I'll go get some clothesline." The laundry room was next to the kitchen, where Nana was baking. Lizzie tiptoed past Nana. She looked around for some new line, but there wasn't any. The only clothesline hung across the room.

Lizzie brought a chair over and stood on tiptoe, trying to untie the line. The knot was tight, and it was hard to force the rope through the loop, but finally she loosened it. Suddenly she heard a gasp, then a little scream, and Lizzie almost fell off the chair.

Nana stood in the doorway. "Oh, my God," she said. "I thought you were a burglar. I heard a noise in the laundry room. You scared me to death." Nana was panting and holding her chest.

"I just needed some clothesline," said Lizzie.

"What are you doing with that rope?" demanded Nana.

"Sara and I need it," said Lizzie. "Mom lets me play with it. I'll put it back when we're done."

Nana stared at her as she went over to untie the other end of the line.

"You can't do that," said Nana. "You can't

just tear the house apart for your silly games."
Lizzie ignored her.

"Stop that!" insisted Nana.

"Mommy says it's all right. Honest. She knows
Sara and I are playing cowgirls and we need a
rope. Mom said I could take it. It's her rope. It's
her house."

"Don't you talk to me like that, young lady. If
I say you can't do something, you can't do it."

Now the rope lay on the floor like a snake between Lizzie and Nana. Lizzie started to gather it up.

"Mom says it's O.K., Nana. I told her this morning that Sara and I wanted to play with the clothesline, and she said I could take it. She'll be mad at you if you don't let me."

Lizzie had the rope wound around her arm. She ran past Nana, holding tightly to the rope.

"Your mother spoils you rotten," Nana yelled after her.

Lizzie's heart was beating very fast when she got back to her room.

Sara was lying on the floor reading *The Black Stallion Returns.* "What took you so long?" she asked, not looking up from her book.

"I had to untie the rope. Come on, let's play some more."

"I don't want to play that game any more."

"Sure you do. There's lots of terrific things still to happen. We get free, and the robbers are about to kill our father and we save him."

Sara looked thoughtful. "I just don't feel like being tied up again," she said finally.

"You could tie me up. I didn't get tied up the last time."

"O.K.," said Sara. Lizzie sat down on the chair.

It had a plastic cover on the seat, and it made a squishy sound as she wiggled on it. "Tie me tight," she said.

Sara wrapped the rope around Lizzie's chest and arms, pinning her arms to her sides. Then she slipped the rope under the seat and wrapped it twice around Lizzie's ankles. She pulled the loose end around to the back and started to make a bow out of the two ends, but the loop slipped and turned into a knot.

"Can you move?" Sara asked.

Lizzie's legs couldn't touch the floor. She tried making little hopping motions in the chair, and the chair moved a couple of inches, but Lizzie remained tight on top of it. She tried wiggling her arms, but the rope cut into her and started to hurt a little.

"O.K.," said Lizzie. "I can't move."

"Now what happens?" asked Sara, walking around the chair and standing in front of Lizzie.

"The robbers go away to get money from our father. I call to my horse. You pretend you're my horse."

"What do I do?"

"You know I'm in trouble. You crash into the shack, stamping and snorting. Then you come over to where I'm tied up and bite through the ropes. Only you don't really have to bite the rope, you can just untie me."

Sara nodded her head.

"O.K.," said Lizzie. "I'm going to call you." Lizzie changed her voice so that she sounded very desperate. "Help! *Help!*"

Sara stuck her lips out and made a sputtering sound, shaking her head vigorously.

"What's that?" asked Lizzie.

"I'm snorting," said Sara, stamping her feet up and down, prancing in front of Lizzie.

"Good boy," said Lizzie, pretending Sara was her horse. "I knew you'd come. You've got to get me loose." Lizzie changed her tone of voice. "Remember, you really don't have to bite the rope, just untie me."

Sara nodded and went around to the back of the chair. "Ouch!" cried Lizzie as Sara pulled on the ropes.

"Wait a minute," said Sara. "It's hard to get."

Lizzie sat still. "Can you get it now?" she asked after about fifteen seconds.

"It's all knotted. I tied it in a bowtie, but now it's a knot."

"There's a scissors on my desk," said Lizzie. "See if you can cut it." Sara got the scissors, but they were a pair of dull paper scissors. She tried sawing at the rope, but the scissors just slipped back and forth, leaving it whole.

"They're not sharp enough," said Sara, working at the knot with her fingers. "I can't get it," she finally said. "I'd better go get your Nana."

"No," said Lizzie. "That would be the worst thing you could do."

"But I can't get it undone myself." The ropes were beginning to hurt Lizzie's arms, but she didn't say anything. Sara came and sat down on the bed, facing Lizzie. "We probably shouldn't have tied each other up, especially with the clothesline."

"It'll be O.K.," said Lizzie. "You just have to get the scissors from the sewing room. They're sharp. Only you've got to be careful Nana doesn't catch you."

"Would she be mad?" asked Sara.

"Worse than that," said Lizzie. "She might go crazy and do something terrible."

"What do you mean?" demanded Sara.

"You know that story I told you about Nana's friend bashing the kitten on the head."

"Of course I remember," said Sara.

"I lied to you. It wasn't a friend of Nana's. It was really Nana."

Sara looked shocked. "I don't believe you. She

killed her own daughter's kitten? That's horrible! You're making it up!"

"I am not. It's a family secret."

"If that's really true and you're not lying, then she must be crazy," cried Sara. "We shouldn't be here alone with a crazy person."

"The best thing to do is just get the scissors and get me untied. Nobody has to ever know we tied each other up. Nana's probably asleep anyhow. She won't bother us."

"I'm scared," said Sara. "Suppose she goes crazy when she sees me."

"She won't," said Lizzie. "She likes you. Besides, she's such an old lady, you can run faster than she can. Please, Sara. It'll be awful if she comes in here and finds me tied up."

Sara looked very upset, but there didn't seem anything else to do except go and get the sharp scissors. Sara opened the door and peered down the hall. She could hear the sound of the television and nothing else. "She's got the television on," she whispered.

"That's a good sign," said Lizzie.

Sara tiptoed past the living room. She could see Nana sitting in her chair; her mouth was open. Sara could hear her snore. She took a deep breath and went into the sewing room. She found the scissors easily and headed back for Lizzie's room. As Sara went past the living room, Nana's head jerked up.

"What do you have there?" demanded Nana. Sara held the scissors pointing toward the floor, the way she had been taught.

"Scissors," answered Sara in a very soft voice.

"What are you girls doing? I don't like all this sneaking around." Nana started to get out of her chair.

Sara bolted down the hall for Lizzie's room. "She saw me," gasped Sara as she flung the door open.

"Close the door," cried Lizzie.

Sara closed the door and put her weight behind it. "There's no lock," she cried, fumbling with the doorknob.

"I know," said Lizzie. "My mom won't let me have one. Quick, get me untied." Sara rushed over to Lizzie. She raised the scissors behind Lizzie's back and started to cut the rope.

"Oh my God!" shrieked Nana as she opened the door. Lizzie sat on the chair, ropes around her chest and feet. Sara stood behind her, the sharp scissors pointed at Lizzie's back.

Lizzie felt her heart thumping. She knew they had done something wrong by tying each other up and that Nana would be mad. Nana looked shocked. Lizzie felt she had to say something, and she said the only thing she could think of: "Mommy says you should knock before you come in."

Nana didn't seem to hear this comment, and just repeated, "Oh my God."

Sara stood there frozen, unable to do anything.

"Keep cutting," whispered Lizzie furiously. Her voice forced Sara back into action. She cut at the tough clothesline until finally the last strings parted. Lizzie wiggled her arms and the rope dropped into her lap, leaving dark red welts on her arms. She kicked her legs free. For several seconds she was the only one moving in the room. Nana stood with her hand to her mouth. Sara looked terrified. Without knowing it, she was pointing the scissors at Nana.

Quickly Lizzie picked up the rope. Finally Nana seemed to recover her voice.

"Oh my God . . . what have you girls been doing? Oh my God . . . I never . . . I never saw anything like it in all my life."

"It was just a game, Nana. We were playing cowgirls and robbers. We play it all the time."

"Don't you start with your stories," shouted Nana. "From one moment to the next I never know what's going on in your head. Wait until your mother hears about this."

Sara was trembling, trying to choke back tears. She was convinced that at any second Nana might go completely crazy.

Lizzie rubbed her arms where the rope had been. It had really hurt. "It was just a game," she told Nana.

Nana shook her head. "I'll talk to your mother about it. Tying each other up . . . sneaking around. I want you to keep your door open. Nothing secret. I'll talk to your mother when she comes home." She turned and left the room.

"I hate her," said Sara. "She's scary. I don't think your mom should have left us alone with her. I bet if my mom knew I was in the house with a crazy person, she'd be mad."

"You can't tell your mom that Nana's crazy," said Lizzie anxiously. "It's a secret. You promised. You crossed your heart and hoped to die."

"I didn't cross my heart," Sara insisted. "I didn't even promise."

"You did too," said Lizzie.

"I did not."

"No, once you promise you can't tell anybody. You promised, and you can't go back on your word."

Sara was furious. She was sure she had not promised, and besides, she was still scared of Nana. "I don't like it here," she said, sitting down on the bed. The sheets and blankets lay all around the room.

Lizzie looked at her, suddenly realizing how upset Sara was. Lizzie felt awful. She wished she had never told Sara that lie about Nana being crazy. She could see now how scared Sara was, but Lizzie didn't have the nerve to tell her that the whole thing had been a lie. And then she realized that she was scared too.

"We can play a game," she suggested, hoping that Sara would quickly forget about Nana.

Sara shook her head. "I don't feel like it. What do you think is going to happen?"

"Nothing," said Lizzie. "You won't get in trouble, and Nana won't bother us."

"I don't think my mom would like it if she knew we tied each other up," said Sara thoughtfully.

"She'll never find out about it," said Lizzie.

Sara picked up *The Black Stallion Returns,*

turned over on her stomach, and started to read. Lizzie watched her, still feeling scared. "You are my best friend, aren't you?" she asked shyly.

"I guess so," said Sara, but she didn't look up from her book. Tears came to Lizzie's eyes. She wiped them away.

Sara read. Lizzie just hugged her knees.

9

A *half-hour* went by, with Lizzie and Sara hardly saying a word. Then they both heard Mrs. Kahn come home, and seconds later Nana's voice saying, "It was terrible. Your daughter was tied up in a chair . . . tied up like a chicken."

Lizzie and Sara exchanged guilty, scared looks. They heard Nana's and Mrs. Kahn's footsteps coming down the hall. The two women filled the doorway. Nana pointed to Lizzie. "Take a look at her arms. They're all swollen and red."

"What's been going on here?" demanded Mrs. Kahn. "Nana's terribly upset. What were you girls doing?"

Lizzie met her mother's eyes. "We weren't doing anything wrong, honest," said Lizzie. "We were playing a game we learned in school. Ms. Cole had a contest for who could think up the best story, and I won. It was the story about two girls who live on a ranch and get caught by robbers. Ms. Cole thought it was a terrific story. She had us act it out in class. Sara and I were just doing what we did in class. We weren't doing anything horrible. Ms. Cole says it's good to use our imaginations."

Sara stared at Lizzie, open-mouthed. Lizzie turned and gave her an innocent look. Sara closed her mouth.

"That girl will try to talk her way out of anything," said Nana.

Lizzie ran to her mother and gave her a hug. "Honest, Mom, Sara and I were just playing, and Nana didn't understand and got upset. We were having a terrific time. We didn't hurt anything."

Mrs. Kahn didn't hug Lizzie back. Her arms hung at her sides as she said, "I think, Lizzie, there is more to it than that. I want to know what you were doing."

"Look at this room," said Nana, pointing to

the crumpled sheets and blankets on the floor. "It looks like a cyclone hit it."

"Nana, *I'm* talking to Lizzie," said Mrs. Kahn sharply.

"We'll clean the room up right away," Lizzie said quickly. She hoped that she could distract her mother so she would forget about everything else. But it didn't work.

"I think things got out of hand here, and I want to know why," demanded Mrs. Kahn.

Lizzie looked up as innocently as she could. "We were playing. I told you, it was just a game."

Mrs. Kahn turned to Sara. "Is it true this is a game you played in school?" she asked.

Sara stammered. Lizzie looked at her, horrified. "Sort of," muttered Sara.

Mrs. Kahn turned back to Lizzie. "Nana says you said I gave you permission to use the clothesline. You know that's a lie."

"I didn't exactly say you gave me permission," Lizzie said defensively. "I said I thought you wouldn't mind. Nana misunderstood me."

"I did not," insisted Nana. "She said you told her to take the clothesline."

Mrs. Kahn glanced at Sara, who was looking miserable. She didn't want to yell at Lizzie in front of Sara or make Sara listen to Nana and Lizzie fighting. "All right," Mrs. Kahn said finally. "You and Sara finish cleaning up the room. Lizzie, I want to talk to you later. Come on, Nana, let them straighten out this mess by themselves."

Nana shook her head. "You play deaf, dumb, and blind," she said.

"I'll talk to Lizzie after Sara's gone," replied Mrs. Kahn as she left the room.

Sara helped Lizzie make the bed. She worked quietly, avoiding Lizzie's eyes.

"See," said Lizzie, hoping to cheer Sara up. "We didn't get in too much trouble."

"That was a lie about our playing that game in school."

Lizzie had hoped that Sara wouldn't mention that. "It wasn't a big lie," she said. "It was just a little lie. We weren't really doing anything wrong."

"I hate it when you get me mixed up in your lies," Sara said angrily.

Lizzie didn't know what to say. She felt miserable. She tried once more. "I just lied to get us out of trouble. You can't tell me you never lie."

"I'm not a goody-goody," said Sara, "but I just don't like to lie."

Lizzie thought about that. She didn't like to lie either, but she did it all the time. Right now, all Lizzie cared about was making sure Sara was still her friend, but she didn't know how to do it. When they finished making the bed, Sara asked, "What time is it?"

"Four thirty," said Lizzie. "We've got plenty of time for another game. What do you want to play?"

"I think I should get ready to go home," said Sara. "My mom will be here soon." Sara gathered up her things, put on her sweater, and sat on Lizzie's bed, reading her book. The silence grew more and more uncomfortable for Lizzie, but she couldn't think of anything to break it. She felt awful. To make herself feel better, she tried telling herself that Sara wasn't really mad or upset. But she knew it wasn't true. Finally Sara's mother arrived.

Sara ran to her and gave her a hug.

"Did you have a good time with Lizzie?" Sara's mother asked.

Sara nodded her head but didn't say anything.

"Did everything go all right?" Sara's mother asked Mrs. Kahn.

"The play got a little wild there for a while," said Mrs. Kahn. "But I think they had a good time."

"Well, thanks for having her," said Sara's mother, and she and Sara left. Lizzie watched them go with a sinking feeling.

As soon as the door closed Mrs. Kahn said, "I want to talk to you."

"What about?" asked Lizzie, hoping she could get away without having to explain what had happened.

"I want to talk to you about the lie you told. I don't like you lying to Nana, to me, or to anybody."

"I didn't think you would mind if we used the clothesline," pleaded Lizzie.

"That's not the point. You told a deliberate lie," said Mrs. Kahn.

"I didn't mean to lie," said Lizzie. She felt shaky and scared inside, but her voice sounded controlled, even hard. She desperately wanted her mother to drop the subject.

Mrs. Kahn looked straight at Lizzie. "You can't lie whenever you feel you've done something wrong. It makes it worse. It's much more dangerous than just doing something you shouldn't. If you keep lying, people will find out and won't trust you. You don't want that to happen. I know you don't. You want me to trust you, but I can't if you're always lying."

Lizzie felt she would explode if she admitted to her mother how much she lied. All she wanted to do was get away somehow, get to her room and be alone. She couldn't even trust herself to speak. She just looked down at the floor, feeling miserable.

Mrs. Kahn sighed. She didn't seem to know what to say. "Sweetheart," she said softly. "It really isn't so hard to tell the truth."

Lizzie shook her head back and forth. Her mother didn't know the half of it. It seemed impossible to go back and erase all the lies. There were just too many. She had to find a way to end the conversation. The only excuse she could think of that her mother might accept was that she needed to practice for the dance Assembly.

"Mom, I really didn't mean to lie," she said earnestly. "It just slipped out. I've been thinking about the dance Assembly so much that sometimes I don't even know what I'm saying. Look, I've really got to practice. It's important."

"I don't want to lecture you," said Mrs. Kahn. "I know how you get when you think you're being lectured. You just close up and don't listen, but I want you to understand that this is important. I know the dance Assembly is important too. It's one of the reasons why I think it's so unnecessary for you to lie. You have so many wonderful things to be proud of. You should be big enough to admit it when you do something wrong." Mrs. Kahn looked at Lizzie in surprise. If anything, she had meant her words to cheer Lizzie up, but Lizzie looked even more miserable than just a few seconds ago. She looked close to tears.

"Darling, come on," said Mrs. Kahn. "It's not the end of the world. You can go practice for your dance. In fact, I've been meaning to ask you—are parents and grandparents allowed to come? Both Nana and I want to go."

Lizzie didn't meet her mother's eyes. "Oh, no," she said hurriedly. "There isn't enough room. This is only for kids."

Mrs. Kahn looked very disappointed. "I was really looking forward to it. Do you think if I called your teacher she could sneak me in? After all, you are the star."

"No," said Lizzie sharply. "It's an absolute rule. The teacher asked our parents not to call. A lot of parents want to come, but there isn't room for any of them." Lizzie was talking very precisely, and her voice had an edge to it.

"You don't have to snap at me," said Mrs. Kahn. "I wanted to go for your sake."

"I wasn't snapping," said Lizzie. "My throat hurts . . . remember, I had a sore throat this morning, and it hurts to talk."

Mrs. Kahn looked skeptical. She hadn't really believed Lizzie that morning, and from what she had heard from Nana, Lizzie certainly hadn't acted sick all day. Mrs. Kahn thought about telling Lizzie she didn't believe her, but then she thought Lizzie had had enough for one day. Besides, perhaps she really did have a sore throat. The one thing Mrs. Kahn was sure of was that the dance Assembly was very important to Lizzie, and she felt that Lizzie was probably much more nervous about it than she was admitting.

"O.K.," she said. "Why don't you go to your room and rest before dinner, or practice if you'd like. But come here and give me a smile and a kiss first."

Mrs. Kahn bent down and gave Lizzie a hug. When Lizzie got to her room she picked up the book that Sara had left on the bed and tried to read, but she couldn't.

10

On Monday morning, the day of the dance Assembly, Lizzie was up early. She hadn't slept well, and she took a shower and washed her hair to make herself feel better. On the way back to her room, Nana stopped her.

"I'll comb your hair for you," she said.

"I can do it myself," said Lizzie.

"Today's such a special day," replied Nana. "I want to help you look nice."

"I want Mommy to do it," said Lizzie, catching a glimpse of Mrs. Kahn coming out of her bedroom.

"I've got to get breakfast," said Mrs. Kahn. "Let Nana do it. She can do a better job with your hair than I can."

"Ouch!" cried Lizzie as Nana hit a tangle.

"Stop moving your head," insisted Nana. "You're so nervous and jerky, I can't do a thing for you."

"But you're hurting me," said Lizzie.

Mr. Kahn came out of the bedroom and passed Lizzie and Nana. "Getting ready for the big day?" he asked cheerfully.

"Her hair will look a mess, and it won't be my fault," said Nana.

"She looks beautiful to me," said Mr. Kahn. "Come on, honey, let's get breakfast." Lizzie slipped away from Nana gratefully and took her father's hand. Together they went into the kitchen.

"Well, today's the big day," said Mrs. Kahn when she saw Lizzie. "I wish I could be there to see you."

"I'd like to see you in your costume," said Nana. "Will you bring it home to show us?"

"We're not allowed to keep them," said Lizzie.

"I thought your teacher was making that costume just for you," said Nana.

"I'm the first person to wear it, but they're going to use it again." Lizzie made it sound as if Nana should have known this.

"I only wanted to see it because you said it was so pretty." Nana sounded hurt.

After breakfast, Mr. Kahn was the first to get up. "Don't worry about that dance," he said to Lizzie. "I know you'll be good."

Lizzie gave him a weak smile.

"Tonight it'll all be over," he said reassuringly as he gave Lizzie a kiss.

"Would you like me to drive you to school today?" Mrs. Kahn asked. "Maybe you're too nervous to take your bike. I'd like to do it. I think you should save all your energy for the dance."

"No, I want to take my bike," said Lizzie.

"Then give Nana and me a kiss for good luck," said Mrs. Kahn. Nana looked at Lizzie. For a second Lizzie felt that Nana was sad, and she wanted to go over and hug her. Then Nana looked back down at her coffee cup, and the lines around her mouth fell into a frown. Lizzie gave Nana a quick kiss.

"I bet you're the best one there," said Nana. "Just remember to comb your hair before you go out."

Mrs. Kahn put her arms around Lizzie. "I'm so proud of you today," she said.

"I've got to go, Mom," said Lizzie uncomfortably.

"Good luck! Nana and I will be thinking of you all day."

Lizzie felt relieved to be on her bike and off to school. When she got there, Sara and Mary were whispering together. Lizzie thought she saw them look up at her, but she couldn't be sure. She knew that Mary was Sara's second favorite friend. "Are they talking about me?" Lizzie wondered. She realized with a shock that she didn't have a second favorite friend. There were a lot of kids she got along with, but there was nobody she was really close to, except Sara.

As Lizzie knelt by the bike rack, she fumbled with the combination of her bike lock, hoping Sara would come over. Lizzie's eyes were glued to the spokes of her wheel. "I'll wait a few seconds and she'll come," Lizzie thought to herself. But when she finally stood up, Sara and Mary had gone inside.

Lizzie stood alone by her bike. Kids from her class went past her, and she said quick hellos, but she felt lost. Hearing the home-room bell, she gathered up her books and went in slowly.

To Lizzie's surprise, her teacher came over and sat on the edge of her desk. She smiled warmly at Lizzie. "I thought the story you wrote last week was wonderful and exciting. I'd like to read it to the class. Is that O.K.?"

"Sure," said Lizzie, feeling proud. "Maybe when Sara hears my story she'll want to be my friend," Lizzie thought. She squirmed in her chair to catch Sara's eye, but Sara seemed to be looking every place but at her.

Ms. Cole called the class to order. "Last week you all wrote adventure stories. I told you they could take place anytime, anywhere, so long as you made the story exciting. I'd like to read you Lizzie Kahn's story because it shows a marvelous imagination. Lizzie makes you want to know what happens next. Here is the story:

"'Once, long ago, there was a princess who was very, very brave. Her father was fighting a war against a nearby kingdom, and he got killed in battle. The queen wanted to surrender, but . . .'"

Lizzie's face grew hot and red. She had forgotten it was *that* story. Instead of feeling good, she felt terrible, as if she would never get out of the tangle of lies.

Ms. Cole finished the story, and everybody

clapped, including Sara. Ms. Cole asked the class to tell why they liked the story.

"It's exciting," said Mary. "It's as good as a story you read in a book."

"I liked the part where the princess gets hurt in the battle," said Sam.

Lizzie began to feel better. Maybe it really was a good story. Lizzie forgot for a second the jumble of lies she had worked herself into, and basked in the praise from her classmates.

The morning went by fast. At noon they all went to the playground to eat lunch. Lizzie stood to the side a little, hoping Sara would come over to her. But she didn't. Lizzie decided she couldn't stand it any more. She'd have to go up to Sara and find out if they were still friends. She couldn't decide whether to ask her directly or to pretend nothing was wrong. Lizzie thought maybe Sara really wasn't mad. Maybe it was all in her imagination. Lizzie took her lunch and sat down next to Sara. Sara said, "Hi," but didn't look up as she poked through her lunchbox and came up with a squashed Hostess cupcake.

Normally Lizzie knew she would have thought of something funny to say about a squashed cupcake and she and Sara would start giggling, but

today Lizzie couldn't think of anything to say. Sara bit into the cupcake, and the marshmallow filling oozed out the sides. Again, Lizzie knew that if this were a normal day she and Sara would be laughing. Instead, they weren't even looking at each other.

Finally, Lizzie decided she had to find the nerve to ask Sara directly, "Are you mad at me?"

Sara's mouth was full, and she didn't answer.

"You seem mad at me," said Lizzie.

Sara swallowed and looked Lizzie in the eyes. "I hate it when you lie all the time," she said.

Lizzie felt as if she had been punched in the stomach.

"I don't lie," she protested.

Sara shook her head. "I always knew you lied, but it's getting to be too much."

"But I don't lie to you," said Lizzie, thinking that the only lie Sara knew about was the one she told to her mother. "I only told that lie to get us out of trouble. You're my best friend, and I wouldn't lie to you." Lizzie hoped with all her heart that Sara would believe her.

"You do too lie to me," said Sara. "I always thought that cat story was a lie. Your grandmother couldn't have done that. It's too horrible. Then I never believed you about what happened to the cat we found. I bet your mom took it to the pound. I never know what's true or not. It gets scary."

"What do you mean, scary?" asked Lizzie, but even as she said the words, Lizzie understood what Sara meant. If it was scary for Sara, it was three times scarier for Lizzie. She was the one who had to keep track of them all . . . remember which lie she had told to which person.

"I can't explain why it's scary," said Sara. "It just is."

"Does that mean you don't want to be my

best friend any more?" Lizzie wished she hadn't asked that question, but the words were out before she could stop them. Sara didn't seem to know what to say. She didn't answer Lizzie's question, and Lizzie didn't ask it a second time.

11

The rest of the day was like a nightmare to Lizzie. She went through the motions, but she couldn't wait for it to be over. At three o'clock she hurriedly unlocked her bike and took off. She passed the half-finished house, and almost without thinking began to look for Princess. She felt that if she found her it would be a sign that everything was going to be all right. She would cradle Princess in her arms, and this time she wouldn't make the mistake of taking her home. She would build a house for her in the vacant lot and bring her food every day. She would tell

Sara that Princess was found, and Sara would see that it wasn't a lie. Together they would take care of the cat. It would be their secret.

But Lizzie couldn't find Princess. Finally she gave up, and went home feeling as if there was no way out of her nightmare. She felt that she couldn't face her parents and Nana. She thought about running away from home for good, but she knew she didn't have the nerve to do it. She couldn't really imagine surviving without her parents, and she didn't want to live the rest of her life without ever seeing them again.

When Lizzie opened the door, her mother rushed over to her. "Sweetheart, we've been waiting for you. I was just beginning to worry. How did the Assembly go?" Mrs. Kahn's voice started to trail off. She could tell at once that something was wrong. She put her arms around Lizzie and said, "Don't be ashamed if it didn't go perfectly. You can tell us. Did you fall or forget part of it?"

"There wasn't any dance," said Lizzie softly, wishing she could disappear into thin air and never have to talk again.

Mrs. Kahn didn't hear her. "Everybody makes mistakes," she continued consolingly. Lizzie thought she saw a look of disgust on Nana's face. She couldn't be sure. Had Nana heard her?

Meanwhile, Mrs. Kahn couldn't figure out what could have happened to make Lizzie look so sad and forlorn. She decided that the dance must have been a total fiasco and Lizzie needed time to get up the nerve to tell her what had gone wrong.

Nana opened her mouth as if to say something, and then closed it.

"Well," said Mrs. Kahn, not knowing exactly what to do or say. She thought Lizzie would find it easier to tell her what had happened if Nana wasn't there. "Nana, can you check the roast?" she asked, hoping her mother would take the hint.

Nana left the room, and Lizzie looked relieved.

"Come on now," said Mrs. Kahn. "Just between us, tell me what happened this afternoon. Whatever it was, I know it's not as terrible as you think."

Lizzie just shook her head dumbly. She didn't trust herself to speak. Only minutes had passed since she first came in, but it felt like hours. Just then, both Lizzie and Mrs. Kahn heard the garage door open. "Your father's home," said

Mrs. Kahn, wishing that he had waited a few minutes so Lizzie would have had time to talk.

"How's my ballerina?" asked Mr. Kahn cheerfully as he entered the room. One look at Mrs. Kahn's anxious face and Lizzie's downcast eyes told him that something was wrong. Lizzie couldn't stand it any more. She felt her stomach get tighter and tighter, and she felt like throwing up.

"There never was any dance!" she screamed.

Mrs. Kahn's mouth fell open. Mr. Kahn just stared at Lizzie.

"What do you mean?" asked Mrs. Kahn.

"The whole thing was a lie. There never was any Assembly." Lizzie's voice was shaking.

"I don't understand," said Mr. Kahn, bewildered. "What exactly was the lie?"

"All of it," said Lizzie, feeling miserable.

Mr. and Mrs. Kahn looked at each other, not quite able to take it in.

"All of it," repeated Mrs. Kahn, stunned. "But, Lizzie . . ."

"You mean there wasn't *any* dance?" asked Mr. Kahn, who was getting over the shock and beginning to feel angry.

"I made it all up," confessed Lizzie. She wanted to run away to her room, but part of her wanted to stay and take whatever punishment her parents gave out.

Both Mr. and Mrs. Kahn were still too stunned to think about punishing Lizzie. Mr. Kahn took a deep breath. "Let's all sit down," he said. "Lizzie, you've got to tell us why you lied all this time."

"I don't know," said Lizzie. "I'm a born liar." It was the first thing she could think of.

"That's ridiculous," said Mr. Kahn angrily. "Nobody is a born liar."

Just then, Nana came in from the kitchen.

"Nana says I'm a born liar," said Lizzie. Lizzie looked up at her grandmother, expecting an angry and disgusted look, but Nana only looked sad and a little frightened.

"Maybe I said that once when I was angry because you lied," said Nana. Her voice trailed off. Then she began again, "But I never thought . . . I never meant . . ."

"Nana," said Mr Kahn. "I'm sorry, but I think this is something that we have to talk over with Lizzie alone. Could you leave us alone for a few minutes."

"No," blurted Lizzie. "Nana can stay." Lizzie couldn't believe it was her voice, but the words were out. Somehow it seemed right that Nana should be there. Lizzie was sick of secrets. When she looked at Nana again she was astonished. Lizzie couldn't get over how much smaller Nana looked than just a few minutes ago, and old, too.

"Nana's the only one who knew I was lying all the time," said Lizzie.

Nana sat down. "I never knew," she said quietly, looking straight at Lizzie. "A few lies, maybe, but not this one."

"I still can't believe the whole thing has been a lie from beginning to end. I just can't believe it." Mrs. Kahn sounded as if she were talking to herself.

Mr. Kahn interrupted. "I think we have to accept that Lizzie's telling the truth." He smiled. "At least that's a step in the right direction. But, Lizzie, why did you do it? And don't give me any of that born-liar nonsense."

Lizzie sat on the couch, mystified. Now that she had finally told the truth, she really couldn't remember exactly how it started. "I don't know," she said honestly. "It just popped out. Mom asked me if anything special happened at school, and I just made it up. I guess I knew

Mom would be happy if something like that happened to me."

Mrs. Kahn looked horrified. "But I love you

whether or not you star in a dance Assembly," she blurted out. "You don't have to tell lies like that."

Something in Mrs. Kahn's voice made Lizzie burst into tears. "It was awful," she cried. "I was so afraid you would find out. I didn't want Sara here because Mom kept mentioning it and Sara didn't know anything about it." Lizzie paused in the middle of her sobs. She thought about all the other lies she had told recently, especially to Sara about the cat. Suddenly she felt angry.

"I really wanted to keep that cat," she said.

"What does that have to do with your lying?" asked Mr. Kahn, surprised.

"I told Sara a bunch of lies about why we couldn't keep that cat, but I really wanted her so badly . . ." Lizzie paused, lost in thought. "You know," she said, surprised because she had never figured this out before, "I lie about a lot of things I want to be true, but they aren't."

Lizzie took a deep breath.

"Do you think you can stop lying?" asked Mr. Kahn.

"I don't know," said Lizzie. She didn't. It had become such a habit she didn't know if she could stop.

"Of course you can stop lying, Lizzie," said Mrs. Kahn.

Lizzie just stared at her mother.

"She needs to be *told* to stop it," said Nana sharply.

No one said anything for several seconds. Suddenly Lizzie knew she had to get out of the living room.

"Can I go to my room?" she asked.

"What are you going to do there?" asked her mother.

"I just want to lie on my bed and be alone."

Mr. Kahn looked at her. "All right," he said. "I think we all need time to do some thinking."

Lizzie closed the door to her room. It was hard to swallow. She could feel her Adam's apple bump up and down her throat. Minutes went by. She opened the door a few inches. She could hear her parents talking, but their voices were too soft to catch any of the words. She closed the door again, and waited for something to happen.

Finally there was a knock on her door.

"The more I think about it, the more upset I am," said Mr. Kahn, bursting into the room. "It was such an elaborate lie and you kept it up for so long."

Lizzie nodded her head; she watched her father pace around the room. He stopped in front of her. "It's not as if you were a little child. You're old enough to stop lying." He sounded angry.

"I'm going to try," said Lizzie. There was just the slightest whine in her voice.

Mr. Kahn sat down next to her on the bed. "I expect you to do more than try. I want you to stop. I've been thinking hard about this. It's not a little problem. Maybe you do it because you're unhappy, or you're angry, but you can't just go on making up lies whenever something happens that you don't like."

"They just come out of me, Dad, before I know it."

"You said that before. I'm not sure it's true. When I thought about it, I realized I can usually tell when you're lying. You get this breathy sound in your voice. But maybe you're not aware of it and you don't know when you're about to tell a lie."

"If you knew, how come you never said anything?" Lizzie asked, close to tears.

Mr. Kahn paused, and the anger went out of his voice. "I guess it was easier to pretend I didn't notice. I thought you'd outgrow it. I don't know . . . that's in the past. What matters is that I want you to stop. I want to help you stop."

"But what if I can't?" Lizzie asked.

Mrs. Kahn knocked on the half-opened door. "Can I come in?" she asked tentatively.

"I was just telling Lizzie that I know it's not going to be easy for her to stop lying," said Mr. Kahn.

"It's not just Lizzie," said Mrs. Kahn. "I've been sitting out there thinking . . ."

"Yes?" said Mr. Kahn.

Mrs. Kahn didn't answer right away. It was so quiet in the room, Lizzie could hear her heart beat. The room felt very small with both her parents in it. Mrs. Kahn looked straight at Lizzie.

"I feel so sad that you lied to make me feel better about you . . . that you felt you had to be a star . . ." Mrs. Kahn's voice trailed off.

"I'm sorry," said Lizzie, looking down at the bedspread.

"Oh, no. I don't mean you should be sorry. It's just somehow I must have made you feel bad about yourself. Like you weren't good enough. And that's not true. I sat there remembering that I used to feel I was never good enough for Nana, that I had to be perfect, and I swore I'd never make my child feel that way. I swore it."

"Sometimes I hate Nana," said Lizzie.

"I know you do," said Mrs. Kahn.

Lizzie looked up and met her mother's eyes.

"What will happen if I just keep telling lies?" Lizzie asked.

"We're not going to let them go by," said Mr. Kahn. "When we hear that breathy sound in your voice, we're going to ask you if you're lying."

"What if I say I'm not lying? What if I want to keep on lying?"

"I don't think you want to," said Mr. Kahn. "Why did you blurt out the truth about the dance Assembly?"

Lizzie thought for a second. "I just felt awful. Like I was going to burst."

"And you felt better when the truth was out?" he asked.

"I guess so. I never thought about it."

"You'll feel better if you stop lying," said Mr. Kahn. "I know you can stop."

Lizzie looked at her mother. "Do you think I can stop?" she asked.

"Yes, I think so," said Mrs. Kahn, leaning over and giving Lizzie a hug. "We'll all try to help you."

12

The next morning at breakfast, Lizzie felt strange. It felt as if everything was different, and yet nothing was. Nana looked the same. Her father was reading the paper. He looked up and gave her a smile. Mrs. Kahn seemed nervous. Nobody talked very much.

Riding her bike to school, Lizzie felt confused. When she got to school, she locked her bike. Sara was in the doorway. Lizzie smiled at her shyly, and Sara smiled back.

Lizzie walked up, not knowing what to say. Before she could think, she was saying, "I've got something to tell you, Sara . . . I found Princess, she's . . ." Suddenly Lizzie heard her voice. It sounded like she had been running, and she felt breathless. "I mean . . ." she said, "I've been looking for Princess, but I can't find her." Lizzie's voice trailed off.

"I thought Princess was in the country," said Sara, sounding a little disgusted.

"That was a lie," said Lizzie softly. "My parents were going to have her killed, take her to the pound. I shoved her off my lap and she ran away. I guess I saved her life. I made up that story about my grandmother bashing a kitten to death."

"I knew it," said Sara. "Yesterday, you said you didn't lie."

Lizzie started to laugh nervously. "That was the biggest lie of all."

Sara giggled.

Lizzie did not dare ask Sara if she'd be her best friend again. Instead, she asked, "Will you help me try to find Princess? She's got to be somewhere."

Sara nodded. After school, they went to the half-finished house, but the workmen still had not seen Princess. They went back every day for weeks, but they never found her. By that time, they were good friends again.